Also by Amelia Littlewood
Death at the Netherfield Park Ball
The Mystery of the Indian Diadem
The Peculiar Doctor Barnabus
The Apparition at Rosing's Park
The Shadow of Moriarty
The Adventure of the King's Portrait

Copyright © 2018 Amelia Littlewood
All rights reserved.
Published by Cyanide Publishing
www.cyanidepublishing.com

First edition
No part of this book may be used or reproduced in any manner whatsoever without the prior written permission of the publisher, except in the case of brief quotations embodied in reviews.

This is a work of fiction. Names, characters, businesses, places, events and incidents are either the products of the author's imagination or used in a fictitious manner. Any resemblance to actual persons, living or dead, or actual events is purely coincidental.

ISBN: 9781980311126

FROM THE JANE AUSTEN NOVEL
Pride & Prejudice

The Shadow of Moriarty

A Sherlock Holmes & Elizabeth Bennet Mystery.

AMELIA LITTLEWOOD

CYANIDE PUBLISHING

We were hurrying to meet with Dr. Barnabus, who had finally agreed to speak to Mr. Holmes and myself about his mysterious employer. At first the man had refused to speak, I believe out of fear for the person who employed him in the first place, but then he had gone to trial and had learned that he was to be sentenced to death for the various crimes he had committed. It seemed that now that his life was going to end in one way or another, he felt more inclined to tell us what he knew.

It was rather grim, but I confess that I was glad that the odious man was telling us what he knew. He had been a disturbing presence in our lives since he had entered them and I would be glad of some answers regarding the attack upon Mr. Holmes and myself. It was sad that the man would have to face death. I was unused to such things, still, despite working with Mr. Holmes and seeing death firsthand and often delivered through violent means, but I knew that I could not spend time worrying overmuch about the man's fate. We all had our choices in life and I could still well remember how he had threatened me and my friend, and quite easily, all for some coin. I fear for my conscience in saying this, but my sympathies were not altogether with him.

The problem, of course, was that now Dr. Barnabus – if he was even worthy of the title of "doctor" (and I highly suspected that he was not) – was destined for the noose, we had a short amount of time in which we might speak to him. There was a scheduled day of execution, of course, but the prisons were

Chapter One:
Dr. Barnabus Speaks

Mr. Holmes and I hurried through the Lon[don] streets so that we might reach our destination in tim[e].

Dr. Barnabus was a criminal, a man who ra[n a] suspect circus of sorts and who had been paid [by] someone – some mysterious employer whom he ha[d] not named – to apprehend myself and Mr. Holmes i[n] order to ransack Mr. Holmes' apartment for information. I had been captured, but had managed to keep my kidnappers occupied long enough for the police to arrive, having been called by Mr. Holmes and dispatched to my location.

It was a close call, I must admit, and it did give me pause about the consequences of working with Mr. Holmes.

But, as my mother had so often informed me with great frustration over the years, I was not inclined to give something up, especially when I found joy in it. I wanted to continue to work with him despite the possible dangers—a point upon which Mr. Holmes and I did not always agree, to say nothing of my family. A part of me wished that I could be a man or a woman born of the lower classes simply so that people would not think that I would faint at the first sign of danger.

notorious for moving those days around and changing the schedule at a moment's notice.

Not to mention that if we had learned that Dr. Barnabus was ready to speak, his employer might have as well. Indeed, his employer might have decided to simply kill him and erase all chance of him talking, whether he suspected Barnabus would speak or not. It all made for a ticking clock for Mr. Holmes and me, and we hurried through the streets. I hoped that my family would not miss me too much – I was sure that they would not, for my first nephew had just been born and I knew there would be great preoccupation with that.

I made a mental note that I must further discuss with Mary, my middle sister, the possibilities that we had touched on about her future. It felt more and more lately as though I were stretched thin between two worlds that both had demands upon my time: my home life with my family that I had always known and to which I still must attend, for I did love my family, and my new life in London with Mr. Holmes. I feared that in living in one I must by necessity neglect the other, and I did not much like the idea either way, for I truly cared for both.

When we reached the prison, it was a dismal scene. Mr. Holmes did not seem to notice it himself. I had found over time that Mr. Holmes did not seem disposed to be impressed by mood or by atmosphere. Everything to him was a series of facts that did not carry emotion. A rainy day was neither calming nor gloomy, it was simply rainy. A sunny day was neither annoying nor joyful, merely warm. I tried to do the same myself and to see things only as they were, but I confess I was still affected by the atmosphere of a place. This prison made me shiver a little in spite of myself, although I did my best to cover it up.

What the poor souls inside must feel like day in and day out, I did wonder and I pitied them. I supposed that it was their punishment for their behavior, but truly, it tugged at my heartstrings to know that people were locked up like this. It just didn't seem to align with human nature.

I told myself that I was being sentimental and foolish. Mr. Holmes showed no hesitation upon approaching the prison, and so neither should I.

Mr. Holmes introduced himself to the man on duty at the entrance. "My name is Sherlock Holmes, and I am a private detective. This is my associate, Miss Elizabeth Bennet. We were summoned here to speak with a prisoner inside. There should be a paper to that affect announcing us."

The guard went through his papers to make sure that we were expected, and then opened the door for us. It was a little like entering a theatre where one presented one's ticket at the entrance, only much less entertaining and certainly not lighthearted.

Another guard met us once we entered and the door closed behind us. "Mr. Holmes? If you'll follow me, please." He paused, looking at me, and I could see the question in his eyes. Being a woman, men that we dealt with, and other women, as well, would often question whether or not I should be involved in the proceedings, especially when it came to matters that were rather gruesome or depressing.

"Miss Bennet is perfectly capable of coming with me," Mr. Holmes said. "She is my associate."

The guard merely shrugged, as if to say I was not going to be allowed to complain if I found the situation unpleasant and began to lead us through the prison. We followed, naturally, and I kept my eyes trained upon the back of the guard. I knew that it would give me distress to see the state of the men around me, and I did not wish to give myself nightmares. This was a world that I had never before seen, one that I had hardly even thought of, so different and removed from my own. Was this the sort of place that Miss Bingley had ended up in after she had arranged for the death of Mr. Wickham? A high-born lady brought so low. She must have been greatly affected by her new environment.

Mr. Holmes was a calming presence at my side. Some people found that Mr. Holmes's constant calm frustrating. They wanted him to become happy or show passion. I found Mr. Holmes's attitude to be irritating only when it led to him behaving selfishly, such as when he left his apartment in disarray. The rest of the time, I found it to be helpful. I could easily become a bundle of nerves in a place like this, but with Mr. Holmes calm and at my side, I found that I could breathe easily again.

We were led through the cold, damp hallways and were finally deposited in a small, dark room that held a creaky wooden table. The guard seemed rather confused as to what to do with me. "We don't get many ladies in here," he confessed to me as he held out an old wooden chair for me to sit on.

I thanked him, smiling as I sat down. It was nice to see that people could still be capable of thoughtfulness and kindness, even in a place such as this.

After we were seated, the door opened again, only this time, the two guards who entered did not seem inclined to hold out a chair for me or anyone else. Their stern faces were understandable when I saw that they were escorting Dr. Barnabus.

The man looked as menacing as ever despite his prison garb and what he must have endured while in prison the last few weeks. I shuddered inwardly when I caught sight of his scarred face yet again. I did feel bad about that, since he couldn't help looking the way that he did, but he had purposefully menaced me and used his appearance and people's reactions to it in order to stalk me and threaten me, in public no less… so I could only muster a bit of sympathy.

My warring emotions of sympathy and anger would not at all serve Mr. Holmes or myself in understanding why we were being attacked. I sat up straight and kept my face carefully blank as Barnabus was seated in a chair across the table from us. He was wearing a set of handcuffs, which I did my best not to look at too much, although it was more difficult than I had anticipated. Having never seen such things in person before my eyes seemed to keep sliding over to them whether I wanted them to or not.

"Mr. Holmes." Barnabus's voice was just as I remembered – I also recalled how much I had disliked it. "And Miss Bennet. You are both looking well."

I didn't say anything, as I felt that it would be impudent of me to speak when I was not sure of what would come out of my mouth. A part of me felt as though I ought to rebuke the man, which I am told I am quite good at doing, but the rest of me simply wanted to shake him and ask why, what business was it of his to meddle with us and scare us and put our lives in danger? What sort of person was he to decide that we were people who were worth attacking?

It was a question that I had asked myself in some form or another time and time again when we were confronted with criminals, wondering what could have made them think that murder or theft was the only option before them.

Mr. Holmes sighed as if all of this was tiresome to him. "Say what you mean to say, so that we might conclude our business with one another."

Barnabus inclined his head as if to say, *As you wish, sir.* "You are wondering about my employer and why I should be asked to go after you and ransack your flat, Mr. Holmes. I must say, Miss Bennet, that there is little use in your being in attendance here – your involvement was merely coincidental as one of Mr. Holmes's associates. My employer's true quarrel is only with the detective." He gave me a rather sardonic smile, and said, as though he were telling a small child to run along and play, "You might as well depart and return home."

I was not to be intimidated by him yet again and I certainly wasn't going to simply get up and leave. While the man's quarrel might have originally been with Mr. Holmes, he had ended up kidnapping me as well, and Mr. Holmes was my friend, with whom I shared a bond, and I would not simply "go home" while he figured out this mystery on his own, especially when such a mystery might pose a danger to himself.

Something of my thoughts must have shown upon my face, for Barnabus smiled as though I had amused him. He then turned to look directly at Mr. Holmes as the detective began to speak. "You told us that you were willing to speak about your employer. Either say what you know about him or her and be done with the matter or we shall be departing. We have not arrived here to play games with you, as much as you seem to enjoy that."

"What can I say, Mr. Holmes? I have a flair for the dramatic." Barnabus gave a shrug and held up his hands as if to say *What can one do?* "It runs in the blood – curse of a performer, I say."

Mr. Holmes was not moved by the speech, for indeed I have found him unmoved by most speeches, despite his deep feelings for humanity. I had found that Mr. Holmes's supposed coldness hid a rather deep and abiding belief in the human spirit. He sought to protect the innocence of it, or at the very least, avenge it, as I had noticed when we were solving the case of Mr. Wickham's death and it was revealed what had nearly been done to my youngest sister Lydia; he sought to applaud it when its resilience was shown; and he expressed disappointment in it when it turned to greed and violence. I harbored a suspicion that rather than being an uncaring man who only saw the facts, Mr. Holmes forced himself to see nothing but in order to spare himself the deep grief and frustration at what he witnessed of the world.

Barnabus saw that his words fell on deaf ears, for he sighed and settled back into his chair. "Do you recall a case that you worked, Mr. Holmes, some time ago – I believe shortly before you and Miss Bennet became acquainted – in which you helped a certain foreign diplomat with the recovery of private papers between him and another foreign power?"

"Yes," Mr. Holmes admitted. "Had the papers been revealed to the leaders of the other nations as the blackmailer involved suggested that they would be, it would have caused an international incident since these two countries had privately consented to several bargains with one another that left other countries out in the cold, so to speak."

"Yes, precisely. In thwarting the blackmailer's intentions, you made yourself a powerful enemy, Mr. Holmes." Barnabus smiled, a creepy thing that only enhanced the scars upon his face. "You see, the blackmailer was a professional in the employ of the same man who hired me to rough you up and take all that I found of use from your flat. He was foiled in his efforts to stir up unrest for his own gain by your meddling, and so he began to observe you. Knowing that he could not afford to deal with you while his plans came to fruition, he summoned me to provide a sort of... lesson in what was in store for you if you continued. I was also to, as I stated, ransack your flat and find any useful information that I could."

"And what is the name of this employer?" Mr. Holmes asked. "And why would he hire a man such as yourself? It occurs to me that there are plenty more skilled murderers at work who he could have hired."

"He appreciated my flair for performing," Barnabus said, spreading his arms as wide as they could go. When neither Mr. Holmes nor I looked the slightest bit impressed, Barnabus lowered them and spoke more seriously. "I am aware of my lower-class state, so to speak, in the totem pole of the criminal underworld, Mr. Holmes. I believe that was my employer's intention. To have a man and a woman murdered by a lower-class criminal would hardly catch the attention of anyone too important, even if one of the people killed was a well-known detective."

"And what is this man's purpose?" Mr. Holmes asked – and surely he must have read my mind, for I was thinking the same thing. It sounded like one of the more adventurous stories I had read when I was a child, of masterminds and powerful counts who sought villainy. But those Gothic novels were merely fanciful stories, and I knew of not a single person who truly believed that any aspect of them was real.

Barnabus shrugged. "I believe that he wishes to accumulate power, but I cannot be certain. I am not one of his underlings. I was hired for one job, and one job only, and I knew that in failing to perform that job my life should be forfeit, and so I am telling you what I know, but it is not much. I know the reason why he sought to hire me to deal with you, and I know that he is a powerful man, with spies and minions everywhere. He is like a spider at the center of a web, they say. The only other thing I know that I can tell you is his name."

I confess that I leaned forward a little, my breath bated. I was curious about this man, and if he even existed or whether he was simply a product of Barnabus's fascination – or a lie the man who had employed Barnabus had told him. It made sense to me that a criminal who had been thwarted by Mr. Holmes should seek revenge on him, but a criminal mastermind? Was that not pushing things too far?

"He is only known as Moriarty."

Chapter Two:
A Difference of Opinion

Moriarty. It was not a name that I recognized, although I had not expected to recognize it. I looked at Mr. Holmes, who showed no flicker of recognition at the name. He simply nodded. "And is that all, sir?"

"That is all."

Mr. Holmes stood and offered his hand to help me up out of my chair. The guards came in again, and the process by which we were brought into the room was repeated in reverse.

Coming out of the prison was like stepping out of the shadows and back into the sunshine. I breathed in the fresh air, a great lungful of it, feeling grateful that I had committed no crimes and would never be placed in such a dreary, confining atmosphere as that.

After a moment, I paused and turned back to see that Mr. Holmes was some steps away from me, apparently lost in thought. I moved to join him and ask where his mind lay. He, as usual, guessed at what I was going to say before I spoke it.

"You are wondering as to my state of mind," he said. "I must admit, I am at a crossroads."

"In what manner?" I asked. "Surely the man must have been exaggerating. This is not *The Castle of Otranto*. I see no ghosts lurking about in the corners of the alleyways and I do not believe that there is one master criminal who is pulling the strings of all the others for some unknown reason."

"Your common sense does you great credit, Miss Bennet," Mr. Holmes said. "And under any other circumstance I should applaud you and agree with your assessment. However, the case to which Barnabus referred to did have some minor aspects that I could never quite reconcile. I had dismissed them at the time, for not all cases can be tied up in a pretty ribbon, as it were, to our satisfaction. Not everything fits in neat little boxes all of the time, for life is a messy thing, as you know."

This was true. Since meeting Mr. Holmes, I had discovered that life was not, in fact, a series of neat and careful categories that I could easily deal with and dismiss in turn.

"There have been other things – I shall have to pool my resources," Mr. Holmes stated. He began to walk back towards his flat and I followed, as always. "But yes. Over the years I have noticed similar little instances and I have always dismissed them. There was always something else to occupy my time, and like yourself, Miss Bennet, I am a sensible person. If the case was solved then why inquire further into a small detail when I knew that I had apprehended the right criminal and all was explained satisfactorily?"

"But now you suspect that there is truth to the man's words?" I asked. "We are to trust in the word of a man who has proven himself to be a liar?"

"A man who is dying soon and has nothing left to lose," Mr. Holmes replied.

I supposed that Mr. Holmes had a right to be suspicious, and this would certainly give him something to occupy his time. Our last case had been done as a favor to Mr. Darcy to help out his aunt, for Mr. Holmes – for some inexplicable reason – held Mr. Darcy in high regard, but it had not been quite as stimulating of a case as Mr. Holmes was used to and I knew that he ached for something that would truly try his talents of observation and deduction.

"Very well then," I said, as we approached the street where Mr. Holmes's flat lay, "where shall we start in our research?"

Mr. Holmes paused, and I nearly ran into him. "Miss Bennet, I cannot ask you to assist me in this matter."

"And why not?" I asked. "I am your associate, as you have been so kind as to remind people that we interview. What should prevent me from helping you on such a large case? Surely a great deal of work is to be done and I can assist you at the very least in doing the research required."

"Miss Bennet, if a criminal such as this Moriarty is truly up and about, then I cannot allow you to accompany me on this adventure. It is far too dangerous."

I rather disliked when Mr. Holmes took on that tone of voice. He had done well most of the time in treating me as an equal but there were times, such as now, when he would speak to me as though he was my superior. To say that I did not appreciate it was an understatement. "Mr. Holmes, I have already been in danger at least once. I'm sure that I can handle any further difficulties that might arise."

"Yes, precisely. You have been in danger once, Miss Bennet, and I do not wish for that experience to be repeated."

We reached 221B Baker Street and began to ascend the stairs up to Mr. Holmes's flat. Mrs. Hudson was not about, it seemed, but for once I was glad so that I might focus on my issue with Mr. Holmes. "I am not a blushing maiden in need of protecting and defending. I am your partner and I wish to be treated as such. What affects you affects me. I am perfectly capable of handling myself."

"Your powers of deduction are serving you well, Miss Bennet, but that does not mean that you are allowed to fling yourself into danger."

"And I think that you are being narrow-minded, Mr. Holmes, in refusing to let me help you. You cannot do all of the research required alone, you will need a partner to help you. I am here and of value to you. You have said so yourself, many a time."

"It is not a matter of whether or not I need your help, it is a matter of my concern for your safety."

"It is my safety, Mr. Holmes. My safety and my life. That means that I can do with it what I choose and in working with you I have chosen to weather whatever storms may come at us."

We paused as we entered the flat and saw that it was not unoccupied.

Sitting in a chair by the fire was a young lady. She appeared to be of wealth and good breeding, with dark blonde hair and a face that was sweet and vaguely familiar to me, as though I had seen her portrait once before and forgotten about it. Mrs. Hudson was just in the process of serving the girl – for she was still a girl, looking to be about the same age as my sister Lydia or perhaps a year younger – tea and biscuits.

"Oh! Mr. Holmes! Miss Bennet." Mrs. Hudson smiled at us. "The young lady wished to consult with you, so I brought her on up. How was your errand? Successful, I should hope?"

"Quite," Mr. Holmes replied.

"Excellent. I'll just leave you to it then, shall I? Lovely to see you as always, my dear," Mrs. Hudson added, laying her hand on my arm in a friendly gesture as she passed me. I smiled back at her and closed the door after her departure.

The young lady stood up and inclined her head politely. "Pardon the intrusion. My name is Miss Georgiana—"

"No."

I looked over at Mr. Holmes. He had interrupted people before – in fact, it was a bad habit of his, and I could tell immediately that his "no" meant that he had observed her and felt that the young lady's case was not interesting to him.

Miss Georgiana looked startled. "I'm sorry, I... I beg your pardon?"

"Please, ignore him," I said. "Mr. Holmes gets into his moods. Tell me, why did you come to see us?"

Miss Georgiana blinked. "Oh. Yes. Well, you see, I have a darling necklace given to me by my brother. He is also my guardian and in charge of our finances, and he has only recently agreed to allow me to return to London following some… trying events during my last visit. I have been watched carefully and I have done my best to behave properly, but then this morning, I found that the necklace – which is very dear to me – had been taken."

"And you wish for us to find it," I said. It was not a complicated deduction.

Miss Georgiana nodded. "Yes. It is of great value, but more than that, it is of sentimental meaning to me. It was the first piece of proper jewelry that my brother gifted me and I wore it when I came out in society. I should be heartbroken if it cannot be found, and I fear that my brother will think that I am still irresponsible and not allow me to attend the season."

For a young lady of our class, I knew, there was little worse than not being allowed to move about in society and attend the many balls and social events that made up "the season" in London. Although Miss Georgiana was young, it was considered prudent that she marry as soon as possible. Many people would begin to look at me as an old maid soon enough if I did not marry – which I currently did not care for, but I knew that I was in the minority. Most ladies were anxious to marry, for it was the only known option open to us. But besides that, the season was great fun for most women and the girl would clearly miss being out and about and going to balls with her friends.

The signs of the young lady's distress were evident in her posture and in her state of dress. I could see several little things, such as the frock done in last year's style and the slight soiling of the hem, that she had not taken care in her appearance when coming here. It suggested that Miss Georgiana had left in a great hurry in order to reach here as soon as possible.

"No, thank you, we are not interested," Mr. Holmes said.

I stared at him. "Mr. Holmes, I see no reason why we cannot."

"We have more important matters to attend to," he replied.

My pride, I must admit, stung. "Ah, but those are matters that you have informed me I am too fragile to take part in. You might not take the young lady's case, but it appears that my time is entirely open, and so I shall take it on myself."

Miss Georgiana looked torn between being pleased that we were helping her and being concerned for the obvious discord between Mr. Holmes and myself. Mr. Holmes turned and looked at me with one eyebrow raised, as if to ask me if I was finished with my childish outburst.

Perhaps it was a bit childish, but I felt that I had a good point to make: he could not prevent me from helping him on this greater matter but then tell me what cases I could and could not take to occupy myself.

"Miss Georgiana," I said, turning to the young lady. "If you would be so kind as to show me the place where the necklace was stolen, I can begin my investigation."

The young lady nodded and started for the door, apparently pleased to get out of the flat where there was such an argument brewing.

I turned to Mr. Holmes. "I will be helping you in the matter of Moriarty," I told him.

"If it pleases you to simply make decrees and expect others to follow in your stead, then you may do so, Miss Bennet."

"Well, why shouldn't I? You do it all the time," I pointed out.

Having said my final remark, albeit a bit of a cutting one, I turned and hurried out the door.

Chapter Three:
A Bright Young Lady

    While part of my taking this case was to spite Mr. Holmes, for I was a rather proud person even though I tried not to be, I was genuinely eager to solve a case and to help out Miss Georgiana. I enjoyed cases for their own sakes and I liked the look on people's faces when we were able to help them. I didn't get to see it as often as I would have liked, for many times the person was too crestfallen by their loss to truly appreciate the case being solved. There is only so much peace one can find in catching a murderer, for example, when one's beloved family member or friend is still dead.

    Miss Georgiana had a small carriage waiting for us, and we climbed in and set off for the nicer part of London town. Indeed, her house, when she told me of its location, was not too far from Mr. Bingley's residence where I was living with Jane.

    "Before we arrive," I instructed her, "tell me all of the facts, as you remember them."

    "I had last seen the necklace the day before last," Miss Georgiana told me. "I had taken out several pieces of jewelry in order to figure out which I ought to wear to my first ball this weekend. A dear friend of mine, Miss Crawford, was in attendance with me. We discussed what would be best for me to wear, and I then put everything away. The only other person with us was my maid, a girl named Rebecca, as she helped us to take everything out and then put it all back again."

Miss Georgiana paused. I noticed how she bit her lip, signaling her inner distress. "Miss Bennet, I do not wish to think ill of my maid. Rebecca is a sweet girl and has always attended to me well. However, I confess that I am aware of great financial difficulties with her family. Her mother is ill and there is a delicate matter involving her brother that has rendered him incapable of working to provide for the family lately."

"You suspect that your maid, then, stole the necklace in order to sell it and take care of her family?" I asked. It was a sensible conclusion to arrive at. I should probably have come around to the same thought if I were in her shoes.

Miss Georgiana nodded. "Yes, but I do not wish to accuse her without evidence. I know how servants talk, and there is always the possibility that another one of them somehow snuck into my room and took the necklace without anyone's knowledge."

"And there is no possibility of it being a burglar from the outside?" I inquired.

"No, for there was no sign of anyone coming in through the window or other strange means, and nothing else was taken. Indeed, everything was exactly where it should be except for the necklace. If it was a burglar, I would think that the person would take more than just the one piece of jewelry."

"That is a very bright observation," I told her. I had often wished, since starting with Mr. Holmes, that people had praised my intellect more while I was a girl. It shouldn't have been such a shock to me that I was intelligent, and yet until my association with Mr. Holmes, it had not even occurred to me that I could be someone of intelligence and capable of deduction and observation. It was my opinion since meeting Mr. Holmes that women needed to be reminded that they were capable of more than they thought that they were.

Miss Georgiana blushed at my praise. "I did not think that it would be fair to Mr. Holmes to come to him without any relevant observations. I know that I can be a silly girl at times, but when one is going to hire a man such as Mr. Holmes, one must show that one is worth his time."

"I do apologize for his behavior," I said. "He has recently stumbled upon a large and complicated case that is consuming his every thought."

"I can see that," Miss Georgiana replied with a smile. "I am glad, then, that you were so willing to take on my case. I admit, I'm a little relieved to be working with a woman. It makes me feel less ridiculous. I know that it is only a piece of jewelry at the end of the day, and my family is not without money. But my brother is dear to me and so is any gift that he gives me."

"My sister is dear to me, as well," I told her. "I have saved every little gift that she has given me over the years, although none so fine as your necklace, I am sure. But I know how you feel. If someone were to take the books that she had gifted me, I would be distraught."

We reached the house, a rather lovely one on a fine, broad lane, quite different from the prison where I had started out my day. London fascinated me in this way. Out in the country, everything was rather on the same level, so to speak. There may be the one estate, such as Netherfield near my own home, that rose above the others in prominence and the wealth of those who lived in it, but for the most part everyone was of the relatively same social status. Great heights of wealth and great depths of poverty were not to be found.

Here, in London, it was all mixed together. There were slums three blocks from the miniature mansions of the upper class. It was confusing and exciting, and made you feel as though you were somehow traveling between multiple worlds that all happened to touch upon one another at the edges.

Miss Georgiana led me inside and up the stairs to her bedroom. I noticed that she was careful not to touch anything, and I appreciated her insight. "I didn't move anything once I discovered the loss," she told me. She then went to her desk and passed me a piece of paper. "Forgive the rambling nature of it, but I wrote down all that I recalled of how the dresser and the jewelry had been before I took everything out and realized that the necklace was missing."

I read the account, and then looked at the dresser. There were several velvet boxes strewn about, with earrings, necklaces, and the like lying either on the polished wood or nestled in their velvet containers. I bent down to examine the lock that would keep the jewelry protected in the top drawer.

It was faint, but I could observe several small scratches around the edges of the keyhole. They were thin, and not many in number.

I stood up again and looked around the room. The washbasin was empty with a fresh jug of water at its side and the curtains had been pulled back to let the light into the room for morning. The bed had been turned down, the pillows fluffed, and some linens were laid out.

"What time did you discover the loss?" I asked.

"At twenty past eleven," Miss Georgiana told me.

"And what are you doing at the time just before?"

"I am an avid student of the piano," Miss Georgiana said. "I sat down for an hour of practice at ten o'clock so that I might finish in time for any morning callers, although I did not have any prior engagements planned. I went over my time, as I often do, and at fifteen past I noticed and decided that I should retire upstairs and plan to go out myself. I went into the top drawer of the dresser in order to pick out a pair of earrings and noticed that the necklace had vanished."

I nodded to myself, and then engaged her in a discussion of the piano while I sorted out my thoughts. Miss Georgiana was a bright young lady and I quite enjoyed her company. But while part of my mind was on her, part of my mind was on the case.

The truth was that I did not suspect the maid. Perhaps another servant, yes, but if so, why not use a key? The scratches around the lock suggested that it had been picked, rather than a key being used, but a servant would surely be able to steal the key from the maid and then return it. It was much simpler than trying to waste time picking the lock.

Another thought nagged at me – if it was a servant, then why steal the necklace in the morning when it would quickly be discovered? The state of the room, from the linens to the bed to the curtains, all suggested that the maid Rebecca had been in to do her morning duties. If she had stolen the necklace, she would not have done those things. She would have needed to get the necklace off the property as soon as possible so that it wouldn't be found on her person. It would have been better to steal the necklace in the middle of her nighttime duties, stoking the fire and turning down the bed for the evening, and then use the cover of night to give the necklace over to her family. By the time that Georgiana discovered the theft in the morning, it would be too late.

"You are certain," I said, interrupting Miss Georgiana's lively tale of when she had tried to play piano for her aunt, "that the necklace was not missing as of last night, perhaps?"

"Nothing was disturbed when I replaced my jewelry at the end of the day," she told me. "I would have noticed then if it was missing."

Then it could not have been the maid. What person could only get to the necklace in the morning, between ten and eleven fifteen when Miss Georgiana was not in her room, and by picking the lock?

A thought occurred to me. Rebecca's financial difficulties might indeed be genuine, but they also made for a convenient patsy for the theft. "Who was it that told you about your maid's family troubles?"

"My friend, Miss Crawford," Miss Georgiana answered. "She told me she had heard about them, and was letting me know so that I might perhaps give the girl a small gift or raise to assist her. I thought it most kind of her to let me know, Rebecca would be too proud to tell me herself."

I nodded. "Thank you, Miss Georgiana. I must say, you are one of the most pleasant clients we've had in some time. I must attend to my own family matters, but give me but a day and I shall be able to tell you who took your necklace."

"I most appreciate it," Miss Georgiana replied. "Come, allow me to see you out. And I hope that you will call again – not in capacity as a detective but as a social companion. I'm in most dire need of an escort and my brother is rather picky about whom I choose after the last one turned out to be not at all suitable. I think he will like you, though, and I would much love to play a duet with you, in any case."

"You will find me a horrible partner," I told her. "I do not play well at all, and that is not false modesty speaking. I am quite awkward."

"I'm sure you will make a good partner, for your company, if nothing else," Miss Georgiana replied. She smiled mischievously. "Do not make me force you, Miss Bennet. I've been told I can be rather a terror."

"Well, now I am quite afraid for myself, and I shall have to pay you a visit," I said, laughing. I was quite charmed by this sweet girl, caught between adulthood and childhood as she was. Perhaps it might do good to introduce her to Lydia and Kitty. My youngest sister had become much subdued since her run-in with Mr. Wickham. Perhaps the three of them would balance one another out and provide good companionship.

I bid goodbye to Miss Georgiana and then proceeded to hurry home. Everyone would be distracted with my nephew, but I knew they would notice my absence eventually – and besides, I hated to be far away from my dear Jane so soon after her ordeal. Childbirth had not been kind to her and I worried that there was still a long road of recovery ahead for her. The prospect of going home, and seeing my family, felt like the perfect way to end this rather unusual day.

If only I had known the kind of welcome that would await me there.

Chapter Four:
Facing the Family

I entered the house in high spirits. I would have to pay a call to Miss Crawford, I should think, and then the case of the necklace would be solved. I had a lovely new acquaintance, one whom I might be able to introduce to my sisters, and I had every faith that I could convince Mr. Holmes to let me help him in the larger case of the supposed master criminal.

"Miss Bennet," one of the servants said upon my arrival, "it is good of you to have returned. Your parents are here and have been asking after you."

I thanked him and then steeled myself. My father would be happy to see me, I knew, and would have no judgment for what I had been getting up to while in London. My mother, on the other hand, I did not have such faith in.

Mary, my middle sister, was in the sitting room with a book by the fire. She looked up as I entered. "Are you looking for Mother and Father?"

"Yes, I suppose they must be up in the nursery, then?"

"Father has gone to take a rest before dinner. I fear the rushed journey did not help in the matter of his health," Mary admitted. "Mother was kicked out of the nursey by Jane."

"Jane? Kicking someone out?" I could not believe it. My sister was the sweetest and gentlest of souls, and would not have a harsh word for anyone, even when perhaps harsh words were warranted.

Mary nodded. "It was done in the kindest of ways, of course, but I could see that she was quite exhausted, and Mama's fussing was not helping matters. She and the baby are both asleep by now, I think. Lydia and Kitty have been taken by Mr. Bingley to pick out some nice gifts for the baby, now that they know he is a boy. Some blue ribbon to put on his clothes, that sort of thing."

"That was very kind of him," I said, and – I added quietly in my own head – very wise. It wouldn't do Jane any good to have people constantly swarming around her and making her more stressed than she already was, and it would do my sisters good to get out of the house. They had always loved shopping. Once, it had been Lydia's chief joy in life, aside from flirting with officers of the regiment. I would have to be sure to thank Mr. Bingley when he returned for this thoughtful behavior.

Mary's gaze slid past me, fixating on something behind my shoulder, and I knew without turning around that it must be Mother standing behind me. Mary's facial expressions were rather subtle, but once you knew them, you could always decipher them, and the slight widening of her eyes meant that Mother had just entered and that she was not pleased.

I turned around and smiled. "Hello, Mama."

"My dear Lizzie." Mother smiled at me and came forward to take my hands and give me a kiss on the cheek. "I heard all about your trip to visit Lady Catherine de Bourgh from Mr. Bingley's dear friend Mr. Darcy."

"I went to visit Charlotte, Mama," I pointed out. "Lady Catherine was kind enough to invite us to dinner, but it was for Charlotte that I visited."

Mother released my hands so that she might wave hers at me. "Do not use your false modesty around me, Lizzie. I had heard from Mr. Darcy about the matter involving his niece and it seemed as though you were quite a part of the whole ordeal. An acquaintance with a lady of that stature—I was quite pleased to hear it."

There was a *but* coming, I could sense it.

Sure enough, my mother continued, saying, "It was such a shock to me to hear that you were much seen in the company of that awful Mr. Holmes. I had hoped despite your letter that an acquaintance with such excellent people would bring you to your senses, but I understand now that was a foolish hope."

I looked over at Mary, who understood at once and rose to leave the room. It wasn't that I didn't trust Mary, for I did, especially after our recent conversation in which I felt I understood her far better than I had before, but this was a private matter and I did not need my mother potentially roping my younger sister in to take sides. My mother was not above using any and all means at her disposal to win an argument, up to and including appealing to others to give their opinion.

Once Mary was out of the room, I turned back to my mother. "I thought I had made it clear in my letter, and you in yours, what our opinions are regarding my continued work with Mr. Holmes. I am not going to give up my work with him, Mother." I should have known that she would not let the matter lie with a simple letter, of course, but I had hoped.

"Elizabeth." Mother looked as angry as I'd ever seen her, eyes blazing. "You cannot throw your life away like this. I simply won't allow it. First you dodge marrying Mr. Collins so that now Charlotte Lucas of all people shall live in Longbourn after your father is dead and buried and I am kicked out—"

"Mother, you have Jane, who has married a very good man, one with five thousand a year. You shall be well taken care of, and I am certain that Lydia and Kitty will find themselves good husbands as well. You have no reason to fear."

"This insolent behavior has gone too far, Lizzie." Mother huffed. "I have spoiled you. I have given you far too much freedom, as has your father. He has always thought of you as the favorite and now I see that I should have nipped your pride in the bud years ago. You would never have treated me in such a fashion if you truly cared about my nerves, Lizzie. Oh, to think of a daughter choosing a life of such ill-repute! This will reflect badly upon your sisters, you know, did you think of that? Did you think of how few men will want them after they hear that their sister has taken up with such as man as Mr. Holmes and is working as a detective?"

"I do not see how my pursuit of such a career will reflect badly upon them," I replied. "And if anything, they are welcome to use it to elicit sympathy from any potential suitors. I do not mind if they complain about me if it will help them to get a husband that they want."

"And what of your father!" Mother cried out. "He worries about you, and what with his health…"

"Father's health is quite fine," I told her. "I know that he gets rather tired on long journeys, but considering his age, Mother, I think that he is quite well. He shall live to see another few grandchildren and his two youngest daughters married, I am certain of it. He has always eaten well and availed himself of a good walk in the mornings."

Mother glared at me. "You are making excuses, Lizzie. This is a selfish and reckless choice and you know it. Do you not think of anyone but yourself?"

"I do think of you," I replied, my own temper starting to rise. "Do not imagine for one second that I do not constantly second-guess the consequences of my actions. But I will not be unhappy, Mother. I will not sit idly by and pretend to be someone that I am not. I will not swallow my words and I will not marry a man that I do not love so that I might survive. Until and unless I find such a man, and even if I do, I shall continue to work with Mr. Holmes because I am finally getting to do what I have always longed for! I am getting to exercise my mind. Mr. Holmes sees me not as a woman, but as a person. He sees my intelligence and does not discourage it."

"You will not be welcome in polite society," my mother warned. "You will be outcast, unable to converse with those you once considered friends, and your sisters shall be obliged to ignore you if they are to avoid being cast out themselves. You are going to drag all of us into wrack and ruin. And there are plenty of lovely young men around you that you can choose for a husband! The love that you speak of is ridiculous, Lizzie, and I did not take you for the type to immerse yourself in such fantasies. You have been reading too many of those Gothic romances."

I should have guessed at what was coming next, given that the more money a man had, the more attractive a gentleman he was in the eyes of my mother, but I have to admit that I was honestly blindsided by her next words. I think perhaps that was why I reacted in the way that I did.

Mother said, "Take Mr. Darcy, for example. He has ten thousand a year, Lizzie, and he is a man of the most excellent breeding. Why—"

That was the point at which I regrettably lost my temper. "Good breeding? Mother, the man is the most arrogant and condescending gentleman that I have ever come across, and I do include Mr. Holmes in that estimation seeing the regrettable first impression he made upon me and often makes to others. But at least Mr. Holmes's heart is in the right place, even if his words can be thoughtless.

"Mr. Darcy upon meeting me insulted me in a most un-gentlemanlike manner. He behaved without decorum, without grace, and treated me as though I were nothing to him! He is rude and proud and altogether the most unpleasant man I have ever met, and he is certainly the last man in the world that I should ever be prevailed upon to marry!

"To think that you have known him but a day and are doing your utmost to set me up with him makes me fairly sick to my stomach! I will hear no more of you trying to set me up with Mr. Darcy or any other man. If I find love then I shall seize it, but I do not need to depend upon a man for my welfare and I am going to keep pursuing that which makes me happy, and that is working with Mr. Holmes, whether you like it or not!"

"Oh, yes, your dear Mr. Holmes," Mother shot back. "And what will you do after he is finished with you? He is not the sort of man who truly cares about anyone else. You may say that I am a poor judge of character, but I know men and I know the world that we live in far better than you do. I have not spent my years upon this earth for nothing, although I know that you think me a fool. Mr. Holmes cares only for the next case and the next puzzle to solve. You are a puzzle to him, that is all, and when he has finished figuring you out and playing his little game of tutoring you, he will abandon you and move on – and then what will you be left with? You will be an old maid, dependent upon the husbands of your sisters, and you will regret not seizing your chance while you had it.

You will be alone and unhappy, and you will have no one but yourself to blame for it."

Fury seized me, and I bit my tongue hard to prevent awful words from coming out that I could not take back. There was arguing, and then there was saying hurtful things just for the sake of saying them and hurting the other person, and I would not give into that temptation.

"Goodbye, Mother. Tell Jane that I shall see her later and that I do not plan to join the family for dinner."

I then – to my shame later on, for it was rather childish of me – stormed out of the room.

Chapter Five:
The Spider

 I hated to admit it to myself and I would never have said it to my mother or anyone else, even under pain of death, but my mother's words had gotten to me.

 I knew that Mr. Holmes could be an overly pragmatic man. To balance out his great feeling for humanity, and his great disappointment with humanity's vices, he adopted a very detached air. He had few friends. Other than Mr. Bingley and Mr. Darcy, I had heard him speak only of one other, a doctor who had gone off to the wars and was currently fighting at the front. I knew of no relatives. Romantic love was something unknown to him.

 And, so, it was not the first time that doubt had gnawed at me. I had contented myself instead with the idea that I was the exception. Other people might come and go from Mr. Holmes's life and he did not care, but I was his true friend. He cared for me and was pleased to have me as a partner. I consoled myself with these thoughts time and again when it felt as though I was nothing more than a sidekick, a wall off of which he could bounce ideas. I reminded myself of the times he told me that my knack with people and my insights were valuable.

But right now, no amount of back-patting on my part could get rid of the fear that my mother might, in fact, be right and that I might be naïve to think that Mr. Holmes truly cared for my friendship.

My mother was, in many ways, foolish. She ignored social cues and was obsessed with finding her five daughters husbands. Or, four, rather, seeing as Jane was now married. But despite all of that, I could not help but remember a time when my mother and I had gotten into a fight – I could not recall what about – and my father had called me into his office.

"Lizzie, my dear," he had told me, "your mother simply wants you to understand that you cannot trust upon the charity of others. People are selfish creatures."

It was true, for I had seen it in the way that criminals behaved when Mr. Holmes and I were called onto cases – and sometimes how the witnesses and victims behaved. I saw people who killed over a pearl, or for a long-standing grudge. I saw witnesses who cared not for the victim or for the crime, but only so far as it affected themselves. I saw victims who fretted about their social standing once it was known that they were burgled, or victims who cared little that their husband had just been murdered. It was, in a way, sickening, and certainly disheartening.

Marriage, in my mother's mind, was the only way for me to protect myself from the selfish world I lived it. But that part was not what concerned me. What concerned me was the idea that she had seen a selfishness in Mr. Holmes that I had not. My concern was that I had been played for a fool.

I reached 221B and hurried up, calling a brief hello to Mrs. Hudson as I went. I found Mr. Holmes sitting in front of the fire in his usual chair, alternately filling a pipe and contemplating some papers in front of him.

"Ah, Miss Bennet. And how is your mother?" he asked.

"Vexed," I replied truthfully. "I suppose that you smelled her perfume on me and noticed the vexation in my own features?"

"Well done," Mr. Holmes said, granting me a rare smile.

I usually blossomed under his praise, glad to have shown my intellect, but now it only served to worry me further. What would he have done if I had not known which observations helped him to reach the conclusion that I had spoken to my mother? Would he have been disappointed with me? Would he have thrown me aside?

"Something is troubling you," Mr. Holmes said. He sat up a little straighter and let the papers fall onto his lap. "I must admit that it is only my long acquaintance with you that allows me to see that it is not your usual quarreling with your mother. Has something else come amiss?"

"You must allow me to help you," I blurted out. "Mr. Holmes, you claim that I am your associate. You must allow me to assist you, then, in finding this Moriarty."

Mr. Holmes frowned at me. "I have told you, the danger—"

"I am afraid," I admitted. "No, I am terrified. I live in terror of becoming what I was before I met you: a bored woman with nothing truly worthwhile in my life. My best friend lives far away and with a fool of a man, and my dear sister has her own husband and child now to occupy her time. I have nothing to satisfy the rattling of thoughts in my mind. I seek to exercise myself and to be useful. I wish to be anything but bored, and I fear that one day I shall be that again, and that it will be because I have failed you and you have no more use for me."

Mr. Holmes stood up, setting his papers aside. "Miss Bennet, if it would not be untoward for a lady to smoke this, I would offer you my pipe to help calm you. I see that your discussion with your mother has worried you more than usual."

I nodded. "I know that it is perhaps foolish of me to doubt our friendship, but I cannot go back to the life that I had before. It would depress me too much."

"Miss Bennet, I assure you, I have no intention of breaking off our friendship." Mr. Holmes smoked for a moment, gathering his thoughts. "I am not, overall, a fan of the fairer sex. I pity them when they are put into powerless positions, but I do not seek out their company. Yet while my first impression of you was to dismiss you, since then you have proven to me to be an example to the rest of your sex, indeed to people in general. I value your handling of people. I know I'm too hard on them. Too brusque. And I value that you don't let me bully you – and yes, I'm aware that I can be a bully.

"I'm not going to abandon you. My friendship is not easily won. I admit that. But you have stuck by me through many trials. You have been willing to put your life on the line for me. I don't take that lightly. I appreciate you and I appreciate what you bring to my life and my profession. My friendship, once gained, remains so."

A giddy smile of relief overtook my features and I sank into a chair. It felt as though I could breathe easily again. "I appreciate your friendship," I said, for I felt it was only fair that I respond in kind after his speech. "And I appreciate what you are teaching me of my own intellect."

Mr. Holmes sat down again and passed me the papers he had been looking at. "If you truly wish to help me in this matter of Moriarty, I cannot stop you. I doubt that an army could put a stop to you, Miss Bennet, once you put your mind to something. Here is what I have found."

"They are letters," I declared, skimming through them.

"Yes. From this Moriarty to Barnabus, and vice versa, as well as some letters given to me by others that I have tracked down who have also been employed by this Moriarty character."

"They do not say much," I said, reading them a little more closely. "There is nothing in here to identify Moriarty. The grammar is impeccable, as is the spelling, but it lacks the vocabulary of someone of the upper class. The handwriting changes from letter to letter."

"I believe he hires someone to write his side of the letters for him," Mr. Holmes noted. "He can then dictate to them. And yes, there is no mention of anything personal, not even whether Moriarty is a man or a woman. I assume man, for Barnabus referred to his employer as such, but one never knows."

"And what does this tell us?" I asked. "A man has hired various individuals for unsavory tasks, but these are all rather low-level criminals committing rather low-level crimes."

"Yes, I doubt that more professional breakers of the law would have talked to me or been foolish enough to keep such letters," Mr. Holmes replied. "What it tells us, Miss Bennet, is that there is in fact a spider. And there is a spider's web. A network. If this network really does exist, all of these criminals reporting to this one man, then perhaps Barnabus is right and this network extends into the upper echelons of society. Perhaps this is in fact a man who can influence countries."

"I still fear that it is rather fanciful," I warned him, "but you are right. Moriarty, in whatever form, does exist."

"And we shall root him out." Mr. Holmes smiled at me. "I hope that you have no other pressing matters? Did you tell the girl that it was her friend who stole the necklace?"

I gasped and leapt to my feet. I had, thanks to my mother, completely forgotten about Miss Georgiana and her necklace. I was supposed to call upon Miss Crawford and now it would be too late in the day. I would be seen as angling for a dinner invitation, a most grievous social error.

"I haven't! I must—" I paused. "Mr. Holmes, how did you know that it was her friend?"

"I know the young lady," Mr. Holmes replied. "Her brother was a client of mine once. She is a sweet girl, but disposed to being taken advantage of. I had heard that she had made a recent acquaintance of a Miss Crawford, and I know that the lady in question is a secret addict of gambling and has many debts to settle at the local gambling hall."

I could not help but laugh. "Even when there is nothing you can observe on a person, you still manage to know more than anyone else about a situation."

"I do try my best, Miss Bennet," Mr. Holmes replied, smiling. "It's best to keep your eyes as well as your ears open. You never know what gossip you overhear on Tuesday that might prove to be useful Friday."

Very true, I thought, and hurried out the door. I could, with luck, call upon Miss Georgiana before dinner time.

Chapter Six:
The Necklace

Now that I knew of Miss Crawford's gambling debts, it made sense to me that she would want to steal the necklace. That had been my original reason in wanting to call upon her before I had forgotten: I had known she had taken it, but I could not understand why. It couldn't have been simply because she wanted it. She could have asked to borrow it or found out who the jeweler was and have one made up in a similar style for herself.

But gambling debts – that was quite a scandal. Men gambled, although it was something that wasn't really talked about in polite society, but women weren't allowed to play cards as anything other than an amusing pastime among friends. Aside from her lack of fortune plummeting her social status, the knowledge that she had entered a gambling hall would make Miss Crawford a social pariah.

The poor woman must have been desperate to rob from a friend, and to blame it on the maid, as well, with that information about the maid's family. That struck me as cruel. A maid dismissed for stealing, even if it couldn't be proven, would have meant no references when she went to find another job. She would have found it next to impossible to get a good job and might even have starved to death as a result. The selfishness of people once again, throwing one poor girl in the way of danger in order to save herself.

I called upon Miss Georgiana, who was eager to receive me.

"Have you news?" she asked.

"Yes, but you might wish to sit down and brace yourself, for it is rather unpleasant."

Miss Georgiana's face fell. "What is it? Has it already been sold off or broken down?"

I sat down with her on the sofa. "I'm afraid that it was not your maid who stole your necklace, but your friend, Miss Crawford."

I explained how it was done: Miss Crawford had called at exactly eleven o'clock, the earliest time that one could begin morning calls while still being polite. Being a friend of Miss Georgiana's and aware of her habits, Miss Crawford had known that Miss Georgiana would be playing on the piano and losing track of the time, would play until a quarter past or perhaps even later than that.

Miss Crawford had entered, announced herself to the servant, and told him that she would wait in the drawing room until her friend had finished piano, and please, no, don't disturb her. No food, thank you, she was perfectly fine waiting with a book.

Once the servant was gone, Miss Crawford could hurry upstairs. Rebecca would have already completed the tidying up of the room, and so no one would be about. Miss Crawford had picked the lock, and in such a professional manner as to leave few marks, which suggested to me that Miss Georgiana was not the first friend that Miss Crawford had robbed in a fit of desperation.

The necklace secured, and everything put back in its place, Miss Crawford would then simply leave the house. Morning calls lasted no more than half an hour, and the servant would have assumed that Miss Georgiana saw her friend, they talked, and then Miss Crawford had left. Why should he mention it to Miss Georgiana, who would have had to pass through the drawing room on her way up to the bedroom and undoubtedly seen her friend waiting with a book?

Miss Georgiana's face fell as I told the story, until she looked completely crestfallen. "But why would she do such a thing?" she asked, in great distress. "And why make it so that I would place the blame on Rebecca? The girl would have been dismissed by a crueler mistress."

"She is lucky indeed," I said, "that you decided you must have evidence before you confronted her. Most people would have assumed she had done it and dismissed her without a moment's notice and without pay or recommendation."

"I feel as though I must give her something," Miss Georgiana said, "Even though she had no idea what almost happened to her. I feel bad for suspecting her."

"It is our first thought, to blame the servants," I admitted. "As to your question about motive, Miss Crawford is a gambler. She has extensive debts that must be paid off. I tell you this despite the scandal so that you might understand what desperate straits she was in."

Miss Georgiana nodded, looking down at her hands in her lap. "Why did she not confide in me? I would have gladly assisted her. I am given an allowance by my brother which could help her to begin to pay off what she owes."

"I think that she was ashamed," I said. "It is hard to admit, even to our friends, when we have made a mistake or are scared. If you confront her kindly, I think that she will return the necklace and you two can work on a solution together."

Miss Georgiana sighed. "It seems as though everyone I know is eager to take advantage of me. Did you know that I was almost married?"

I shook my head. "Forgive me, but you seem rather young to have nearly married already."

"It is true, I was too young. It was nearly two years ago, now, and I was barely fifteen. I had not even had my proper coming out, which was scheduled for the beginning of the upcoming season. My father, you see, had a steward who was a brother to him, and the steward had a son who was practically raised as a brother to my own brother, Fitzwilliam. But the son of the steward was greedy. At some point, he found me in London and charmed me into thinking that he loved me, and when he proposed marriage, I accepted."

Miss Georgiana gave a self-deprecating laugh. "I thought of myself as in love with him, but he was a rake and I was just a child. My dear brother has been most patient with me in this matter. I thought that he would scold me terribly for my foolishness, but he was as gentle as one could hope for. He raised me, you know, after my parents both died young. I could not ask for a better guardian."

"I can understand why losing the necklace that he gave you, then, was so distressing for you," I said.

Miss Georgiana nodded. "Yes. I did not fear his anger, but more I feared losing something precious that he had given me."

"And how did your brother discover the ruse?" I asked. "It seems to me to be something that your rake would take great pains to keep secret."

"Mr. Wickham – for that was his name – did indeed instruct me to not to tell my brother." Miss Georgiana paused and looked up at me. "Are you quite all right, Miss Bennet?"

My mouth had dropped open upon learning the name of the rake. Mr. Wickham – but then that must mean, from what I knew of Mr. Holmes and of Mr. Darcy… "Your last name is Darcy, is it not?"

"Why, yes," Miss Georgiana gave a small laugh. "Oh dear, I was interrupted by Mr. Holmes before I could give my last name. I had been wondering why you were calling me Miss Georgiana rather than Miss Darcy."

"It was quite rude of me," I admitted, "but I was too embarrassed to ask for your last name. I feared I had simply forgotten it."

"It is no matter, you may continue to call me Miss Georgiana." She smiled at me. "Are you acquainted with my brother, then?"

"Yes, indeed I am, as well as the man who found you for him and helped to settle things with Mr. Wickham," I said. "Mr. Holmes was that man."

"Indeed, was he?" Now it was Miss Georgiana's turn to look surprised. "Oh, I must thank him. Or have you thank him for me. I never met the man, for he did his work privately and then gave my brother information as to where we were, and my brother came directly to us. I felt like such a child when all was revealed to me."

"It must have been rather a scene," I replied, thinking back to what I knew both of Mr. Darcy and of Mr. Wickham.

"Indeed so. Mr. Wickham continued to profess his true love for me, until my brother informed him that I should not see a penny of my inheritance. Nothing that was intended to be mine would pass into Wickham's hands upon his marrying me. After that, he was quick to disavow all promises he had made to me and quit himself of our company. You can easily imagine the distress that I was under." Miss Georgiana shuddered. "I am equally glad that I did not give into his requests that we behave as man and wife. I said that we must wait until we truly were married in the eyes of the law, as was right, and now I am most glad for it, for I would have been a ruined woman otherwise."

"People see a girl with a good heart such as yourself and they try to take advantage of it," I said. "That is true. And it is disheartening. But you have a good head on your shoulders as well. Balancing your sensibility with your sense will help you get far and while it may mean that people try to take advantage, it also means that they will not succeed."

"I only wish that there were people that I could trust," Miss Georgiana replied. "I shall help Miss Crawford, indeed I must, for I do not wish such a feeling of desperation and entrapment upon anyone. But how can I trust her after this? I cannot. She cannot be as dear to me anymore, and that distresses me greatly."

"I hate to sound as though I am promoting my own family," I replied, gentling my voice, for the girl seemed to be near tears, "but I have two sisters who are of an age to yourself. In a full confession, I have to tell you that were we speaking a year ago I would not recommend them to you. They were silly girls who were rather too obsessed with men, particularly men in uniform. But since then, they have matured and gentled. I think that you three would make good companions to one another. If you will allow me, I may introduce you?"

Miss Georgiana smiled. "Thank you. You are most kind, Miss Bennet. I should like to have some acquaintances upon whom I can really rely. But tell me, how did you come to meet Mr. Holmes and my brother?"

"Mr. Holmes was with my sister's husband when they attended the same ball that I did, for they are good friends," I explained. "Although at the time, my sister and her husband had yet to meet. While at the ball, we all made one another's acquaintance and there was a horrible murder. The victim, in fact, was Mr. Wickham, with whom we are both unfortunately familiar. It seemed that his habit of making a victim of women such as yourself had caught up with him and someone had taken revenge.

"I shall not go into further details, of course, as it is distressing, but suffice to say that I helped Mr. Holmes in his investigation and he took me on as an associate. Then just a short while ago, I made the acquaintance of your aunt and cousin when, upon your brother's recommendation, Mr. Holmes and therefore myself were brought in to settle another mystery. I must also add that your brother and I are the godparents of my nephew. My sister, Jane, is married to your brother's friend, Mr. Bingley."

"Oh!" Miss Georgiana let out a small gasp. "But of course! My brother has talked greatly about Mr. Bingley's young son. My brother is enamored of him and I think shall spoil him quite rotten."

"He shall have to get in line behind my mother," I replied.

"But this is wonderful!" Miss Georgiana smiled at me as bright as the sun. I could not find it in me to admit to her that I found her brother distasteful. "My brother is such a good friend to Mr. Bingley, and I know that he was rather worried when he learned that his dear friend was to marry a woman who was of such lower standards than himself. But he must have changed his mind upon meeting you, especially if your family is as lovely as you are."

Again, I did not have the heart to tell her otherwise. But a part of me did wonder...if perhaps I had been wrong about Mr. Darcy?

He had behaved rudely to me, there was no denying that. But he had raised such a lovely young woman, a woman who was smart and sweet of heart and who was utterly devoted to him. And Mr. Holmes had agreed to help him, which I supposed I should have taken into consideration beforehand.

Could it be that perhaps I had misjudged someone too hastily once again? Mr. Holmes and I had not gotten off to the best of starts, and now I venture to say that he was my friend. It did not seem to me that a man such as I had thought Mr. Darcy was could raise a young lady as sweet and thoughtful as Miss Georgiana. Or, if he had, it seemed to me that she would have blossomed in spite of him and would not have been praising him so highly.

"I certainly hope that we are esteemed in the eyes of your brother," I told her, "if only because he has raised such a delightful young lady, and must be commended for that."

Miss Georgiana blushed. I resolved to introduce her to Kitty and Lydia, so that the three of them might begin to find true friendship. Perhaps even, in time, Lydia and Miss Georgiana would be able to take solace in one another's trials, and share their experiences with Mr. Wickham. I could not know, for I had never been treated in the fashion that Mr. Wickham had treated either of them, but I could imagine that talking to someone who had been through something similar could only help.

I stood, and we curtsied to one another. "I'm afraid I must be going," I said. "It is late, and my family will expect me."

"Please do call again soon, as a social visit," Miss Georgiana asked me. "And bring your sisters that you mentioned."

"I shall."

We left one another, and I set off for home, all the while cursing myself. When was I going to stop making erroneous assumptions about people and then turn out to be mistaken?

Chapter Seven:
Truce

I returned home in rather sorry spirits. One might even say that I was feeling bad for myself and my own misjudgment. I had known that I could be hasty in my own prejudices. Perhaps in working for Mr. Holmes I had grown too proud of myself and my observational skills.

Still, it was difficult to reconcile the man that Georgiana spoke of with the man who had made such rude insinuations about my family. How could they be one and the same? The same way that I could be both a good detective and a horrible daughter, I supposed, at least in the eyes of my mother. I confess that I did not know what to do about her. How could I give up this exciting life that I had found with Mr. Holmes? And yet how could I disappoint my mother?

I had just reached the threshold of Jane and Bingley's house when I was stopped on the street. "Miss Elizabeth."

For a moment I was concerned. The last time that I had been stopped on the street by someone, it had been the scarred man, the so-called Dr. Barnabus. He had done it purely to intimidate me, I was certain. But this was Mr. Darcy. He might have been rude, but he was a gentleman and I did not fear whatever he had to say.

"Miss Elizabeth," he repeated, coming up to me. "I apologize for calling upon you in such a manner. It is most unusual of me."

"I should think so," I replied. I realized that I was being harsh again and I tried to amend myself. "Is there a matter of urgency?"

Mr. Darcy shook his head. "Not as such. That is, there is no danger to anyone or anything of that sort. I only wished to catch you so that I might apologize as soon as possible."

I found myself nearly gaping at him and I hastened to school my features into something more calm and unflappable. I was supposed to be a lady and a detective, after all. "What do you mean, sir?"

"Do not trifle with me," Mr. Darcy replied. "I know that you are not unaware of how rude I was when we first met at my aunt's estate. I spoke unpardonably of your family and I now seek to apologize for my words. I confess that I did not hold you in high esteem. Your sister I found to be gentle and kind of heart, but I thought her an anomaly and that all the rest of your family must bring ruin to my dear friend Bingley. But then I overheard your conversation with your mother—another fault, to which I must confess, but I might add that it was quite by accident. I had left a book in the room and had intended to go and retrieve it, only to find that you two were in the middle of your heated discussion. I could not see of a way to leave without drawing attention to myself and so I paused until you parted from the opposite door and I could escape."

I was quite confused about all of this. "You mean to say that you heard everything?" And he did not judge me further?

"Yes." Mr. Darcy nodded. "And I must apologize to you. I was impressed to say the least when I heard from the both of you that Mr. Holmes had taken you on as an apprentice. You see, you may not be aware of it, but a while ago my sister was nearly in the clutches of an odious man. He had once been loved by our father, but he had become greedy and selfish. He sought to marry my sister and thereby obtain her rather large inheritance. Mr. Holmes found this man and separated him from my sister before damage could be done, and returned her to me safely. I owe him a great debt. And then he has helped my aunt, and through both his work and, I suspect, yours, my cousin has at last found peace. I cannot place a great enough amount of praise upon him."

"Why are you telling me this?" I asked. "I am aware of Mr. Holmes's great faculties, which is why I asked him to take me on as an apprentice. But I confess that I fail to see how in citing Mr. Holmes's work, it connects to your realization that you must apologize to me."

"Mr. Holmes took you on as an apprentice and as a partner," Mr. Darcy said. "I know that he would not have done this if you were not an intelligent woman who was worthy of his esteem. He pities women, and seeks to help them, but I have never seen him voluntarily take a woman's company. Far from romance, he seems to even eschew friendship with them. Yet he has made an exception for you. He has not only made a friend of you, but is instructing you in his hard-won talents at observation. I must admit that I myself do not possess his gift. I would not venture to say that I am a stupid man. I am an intelligent one. I do not possess what he does – yet you do. You have it, and he has seen it, and has seen fit to instruct you in things that until now only he knew.

"It says much to me, Miss Elizabeth, of who you are. You must be a rare woman of extraordinary character for him to make a friend of you. Even more so for him to instruct you as he does and trust you as he does. That speaks volumes to me and I realize how I must have misjudged you. Furthermore, I confess that I was impressed in how you stood up to your mother. It is difficult, is it not, for us to go against the wishes of our parents? I know that it was a struggle for me to admit to myself that I could not follow through on my mother's wish that I marry my cousin. You showed great backbone and conviction and I admire that.

"What I am saying, Miss Elizabeth, is that I am sorry. You are well-liked by everyone who knows you. You are held in high regard by a man whose opinions I greatly respect. And your own behavior has shown you to be someone that I should hold in esteem. And so, please, accept my apology for my own assumptions and prejudice."

I was overcome. I had not expected that Mr. Darcy, or truly any man, would admit to having been wrong and in so grievous a fashion. I was unused to this and at first was not sure as to how I should reply. Then I remembered my own failings.

"I must apologize as well," I admitted. "I, too, fell folly to prejudice and my own pride. I fear that I am too hasty in my assumptions at times. I take my powers of observation and I use them to form unjust opinions of others. In my pride, I refused to see you as anything other than a horrible man, even when I had evidence that showed me how wrong I was. I think that we have equally misjudged one another through our own folly. Perhaps we can make a mutual apology and agree to move forward anew. I suspect, after all, that we shall be seeing much of each other given your closeness to Bingley and my affection for my sister."

"A truce, then?" Mr. Darcy said. His lips quirked upwards into a smile. It was the first that I had ever seen from him, and I was surprised at how it made him look much less severe.

"A truce," I agreed. I held out my hand for him. He stared at it a moment, surprised, but then he took it and we shook on it as equals.

"I must say," Mr. Darcy said after we dropped our hands, "that your mother was wrong in one thing. Say that Mr. Holmes did tire of you. I do not think that he will, for he is a loyal man with his chosen few. But say that he did, that would not be the end of things for you. The things that you have learned and that he has taught you, they cannot be taken away from you. He is the only detective of his kind in London. I am sure that there would be others in need of his services since he cannot take on every case, and, as I understand it, is often rather picky with the ones that he does take on."

"Yes, he is," I admitted. "In fact, he refused to take your sister's case when she came to us the other day. I took it on instead and settled the matter for her. It was through her praise of you that I realized my own misjudgment of you."

"Then I owe her a debt of gratitude, and of course to you for helping her. Although, if we may be honest, my sister, I am sure, holds a biased view of me seeing as how I have practically raised her since the death of our parents. She is much younger than I am, as I am sure you have noticed, and I fear I am more father to her than brother."

"I do not see anything wrong with that," I pointed out to him. "Your sister seems an excellent judge of character to me. Perhaps that was a good thing that came out of her ill escapade with Mr. Wickham. She will not be taken in so easily again."

"Thank you," Mr. Darcy said. "She needs more friends like you in her life, people who care for her simply as she is and not for her wealth. But Miss Elizabeth, back to the matter at hand. Your mother threatened that Mr. Holmes should grow tired of your presence and throw you out, so to speak, and that then you should be left alone and friendless and a spinster with no purpose. I merely wanted to point out that this might not necessarily be the case. There are plenty of people out here that you could help. If Mr. Holmes did leave you, you could always open your own detecting services."

"I could?" I felt foolish for it, but the idea had honestly not occurred to me. I think that it was that as a woman I had been raised to depend upon a man for things, whether it was my father or my future husband. It was not yet instinctive in me to think of depending upon myself and being independent, as much as I wanted to be that way.

"Yes," Mr. Darcy affirmed, nodding. "You would need a male partner to put his name over the door, so to speak, if only so that people would believe it credible and attend. But that person need only be a silent partner, someone whom you trust and who would lend you his name. That doesn't mean that you would have to give anything over to him or that he would take over in any way."

"That is certainly food for thought," I admitted. "I would like the idea of such a thing, if in the future Mr. Holmes and I are not able to work together. However, I hope that we do continue to work together for some time and that I will not have to worry about such a matter."

"I hope so as well," Mr. Darcy assured me. "I only wished to inform you of the idea so that you might remember that you are not so helpless as you think. Your mother is scared for you, I know, because she loves you, and perhaps with this information you can help her to see that you are capable of taking care of yourself no matter what might happen in the future."

"Thank you," I said, and I truly meant it. It was a possibility that I had not thought of – but also, what he said about my mother struck a chord with me. I would have to go inside and speak to her. "With all honesty, Mr. Darcy, I do thank you. I hope that we shall be amicable and friendly with one another in the future."

"As do I, Miss Bennet. I rather look forward to seeing you about." With that, he bowed and turned to walk back the way that he had come.

Chapter Eight:
Plucking the Strings

I entered the house, not without some misgivings. I had no idea what I should find and if my mother had perhaps not turned the entire family against me in regards to my detecting. It wouldn't be the first time that she had rallied everyone into stopping me from doing something of which she did not approve.

However, for the most part, things were silent. I inquired with the servants and found that Mary, Kitty, and Lydia were out at a ball, that Jane was upstairs in the nursery with her child, and that Bingley was speaking with my father in the library. My mother, I soon learned, was attending on Jane and her grandson.

It came as no surprise that my mother planned to dote upon him. He was her first grandchild, and a boy to boot. Of course she would lavish upon him all of the devotion and praise that my mother could muster, which was quite a lot. Lydia had been rather spoiled by our mother, but fortunately, Jane and Bingley would prevent the same from happening to their son. And besides, what baby with such loving and gentle parents could be anything but loving and gentle in his own turn?

I made my way up the stairs and tried to think about what I would say. I didn't want to fight with my mother again, really I didn't. But I didn't want to give up any ground, either. It was my life and I had to make my own decisions. Yet how was I supposed to convince my mother of that when she was always of the opinion that she was right and everyone else was merely suffering under a delusion?

I thought again over what Mr. Darcy had said, that my mother was scared for me and that she loved me. Perhaps… perhaps if I showed her that I understood, perhaps if I found a way to assuage her fears, she would be more open to letting me follow my own path. After all, my mother could be rather bullheaded herself. She had been determined to marry my father and she had gotten him. She had been determined to do a great many things, in fact, and every time she had succeeded in getting what she wanted. Was this not how I myself was? Were we not, in fact, alike in this way? My father certainly wasn't known for his stubbornness. He was more known for his contrariness. He tried to avoid conflict and would quietly go about his own business and he gave into my mother far more often than he should.

Perhaps all of this time I had gotten my pride and my stubborn nature from my mother, and I had simply refused to see it.

I reached the door to the nursery and knocked quietly. My mother opened the door, and I saw beyond her that Jane and the baby were asleep together.

"I was hoping to speak with you." I whispered, trying not to disturb my exhausted sister.

Mother nodded and quietly exited the room, closing the door in silence behind her. We walked down the hallway until we reached my room, and waited until we had entered and I had closed the door before speaking.

"I wanted, first, to apologize," I said, wincing. Apologizing to people still pained me, and it felt as though that was all I had been doing that day. "I did not consider how deeply my actions would affect you. I know that you love me and I've never doubted that — although sometimes I admit that I doubt that you like me, if that makes sense. But allow me to assure you, Mother, that I understand that this comes from a place of caring for me and that I would never doubt that is from where your concern stems."

"Oh, Lizzie," my mother sighed.

"I'm not quite finished yet," I said, gently, trying to soften my harsh tone. I took a deep breath. "I have to admit to you that I have not been fully honest with you, because I have not been fully honest with myself. I pretend that I do not need you because you have always stood opposed to me and I do not wish to admit that I need someone who does not approve of me. I tell myself that I can care what-all for someone who holds no respect for me.

"But the truth is that I do care. I care greatly, Mama. I want your love and I want you to accept me for who I am. I assure you that I am not asking you to agree with me on every little thing. You are not a doormat and I doubt you ever shall be. I am only asking that you accept that I am who I am, and that doing this work with Mr. Holmes makes me happy.

"I know that you might not approve of it in every way. But can you not at least accept that whether it was the future you planned out for me or not, it is ultimately what makes me happy?"

Mother sighed and I held my breath, waiting to see what her answer would be. For the first time, I saw my mother actually take her time and organize her thoughts, weighing her words before she said them. It was truly a miracle, or as close to one as I could get.

Eventually, she spoke. "Elizabeth, you are dear to me. It is true that we have not always got along. I will admit that. But I hope you will not doubt that I do love you. You've always been such a lively one. You brought such joy into the house. You seemed to take delight in everything that you saw. Jane was a sweet baby, but I never knew that children could have such energy until you came along.

"I have to tell you that I am scared, Lizzie. I know of women who have hobbies. Some gentlewomen write books, after all. But this is something that puts you in the path of danger and takes you off the path of propriety. I fear what may happen. Consider what nearly happened to Lydia, and the fate of Mr. Wickham. What should happen if something of one of those natures should happen to you? How should I ever recover from losing one of my children in that way?

"I know that you think that I go on and on but Lizzie, you are not a mother. You have no idea the kind of love that I possess for you. It would tear me apart to lose you or any of your sisters. When poor Lydia—" My mother cut herself off, unable to continue.

I wanted to go to her, to hug her, but I was unsure suddenly of the right way to comfort her. When it came to Jane or my father, I always knew what to do to make things better. My mother and I had never had that kind of connection. Would she appreciate my hugging her? Or would she like me to keep my distance? Should I say something? Or keep silent? My thoughts were all in confusion.

Mother took a deep breath and I saw that there were tears in her eyes. "Lizzie, come here."

I came, and she put her arms around me. I hugged her back. I hadn't hugged my mother in years, not since I was very young and became terribly frightened by a thunderstorm. That must have been when I was five or so. My mother and I hadn't been close in that way and she had quickly been swept up in raising my younger sisters. I learned to turn to Jane for comfort and to deal with my troubles on my own.

"My darling girl, I'm afraid for you, that's all," my mother admitted. "I can't protect you from the world. I can't take care of you. And here you are flinging yourself out into it as if you're invincible. And you're terribly smart, and you're terribly witty, and I know that you are terribly brave, but you are not immortal. It makes me so scared to think that you will come across something that can hurt you and can take you away from me, and I can't do anything about it."

"I am sorry, Mother, truly." I hugged her tightly. "I did not mean to do this to frighten you or to flaunt my independence. This is what makes me happy. It's not simply a rebellion against you. I want to have this be a part of my life. Can you accept that? I will try to be careful, truly I will, and I know that Mr. Holmes is always thinking of my safety. But I must do what makes me happy, otherwise what is the point of living? What is the point of life if not to live it?"

"You sound like your father," Mother said, pulling back. She took my face in her hands and smiled up at me, her eyes wet. "Oh, Lizzie. Whatever am I going to do with you, Lizzie? How many times have I said that to you? You do vex me so. You give me so many reasons to worry, and you always have."

"I don't try to," I said, genuinely contrite.

"I am starting to realize that," Mother replied. She gave me a watery smile. "You really are determined to see this through, aren't you?"

"I am. I'm sorry, Mother. I know it's not the answer that you want to hear."

"But it is the answer that I have to accept." Mother sighed. "Very well. Do as you like. All I ask is that you be careful, alright? Please, think of your poor mother's nerves and don't go throwing yourself into danger unnecessarily."

"I will do my best, I promise," I said, and I meant it. After all, Mr. Holmes had made it clear enough that he did not want me hurt either and that he would not appreciate my flinging myself into the path of danger any more than my mother did.

"Good. Now. Shall I see about dinner? It is getting a bit late."

"A wise decision."

For the first time in my life, I felt as though my mother and I had come to an agreement. We were not of an accord, so to speak. Our opinions still differed. But like with Mr. Darcy and myself, we had come to a kind of truce. Perhaps this would mean that in the future, things would be easier between us. I couldn't be certain, of course, but I could hope.

The next morning, I arose bright and early with the determination to head to see Mr. Holmes. I was a little concerned that he would once again try to tell me that it was too dangerous for me to continue to work with him on the Moriarty case, given the circumstances, and I was fully prepared to go toe-to-toe with him about it once again – and as many times as it would take. I was not going to falter in the face of possible danger.

I did feel a bit selfish in thinking this, especially when I recalled how my mother had hugged me last night. I wanted to stay safe for the sake of my family's happiness, but I could not deny what made me happy and I could not stand idly by while my friend put himself in the path of danger and I did nothing. Besides, we had little to go on at the moment. It could do no harm to help in researching this Moriarty and finding out more about him.

Mr. Holmes was in an excitable mood when I arrived. I noticed that his flat was not in its usual state of disarray. Instead, he had shoved everything on one wall to the side so that he might begin to use it to pin pieces of paper and lines of red string to it. The overall effect was such that it made him look rather unbalanced, and had I not known that my friend was the picture of sanity, and indeed more sane than most people I had met, I should have been concerned for his health. Indeed, even a passing acquaintance would have been disturbed at the frenzy with which he was conducting his organization.

"Miss Bennet!" Mr. Holmes turned and greeted me. "Come, you must take a look. I have begun with the help of my homeless network to spy upon those I had a feeling might be connected to Dr. Barnabus and therefore Moriarty. I have also begun to further investigate such cases that I thought might be connected to Moriarty's handiwork – cases that otherwise were unsolvable or solved unsatisfactorily by the police."

I stared at the board before me. "This is most impressive," I admitted. "And to have gotten it done in such a short frame of time, Mr. Holmes. You're most determined on this case."

"I have never before seen such a potential adversary as this Moriarty," was Mr. Holmes's answer. "To face down a true mastermind is a rare treat for one with an intellect such as ours."

Privately, I was inordinately pleased that Mr. Holmes thought to include my intellect at a level with his. It reaffirmed that I was on the right path in my life and that I would not be persuaded otherwise. However, I did frown when I saw the sheer amount of papers and such that were piled up in front of the wall to be nailed upon it. How much information were we going to have to sift through?

"And you are quite certain, Mr. Holmes, that all of this is connected to Moriarty?" I asked. "Some of these seem rather out of one's ability to manipulate. After all, you name several members of royalty on here and some other rather influential members of society. Is it truly possible that one man can stretch so far as to manipulate all of this?"

"With the right motivation and a proper exercising of one's intellect, Miss Bennet, the possibilities of what one can achieve are limitless." Mr. Holmes spoke with his usual conviction. Mr. Holmes was usually right about such things and so one can understand and forgive him for thinking that he was always correct in all things. I was not so certain.

"But what if this turns out to be a wild goose chase?" I asked.

"Are you doubting that Moriarty exists?" Mr. Holmes asked me, incredulous. "We have already begun to discuss how his handiwork can be found if one knows where to look. We have seen his correspondence with Dr. Barnabus."

"Be that as it may, Mr. Holmes," I replied, "I speak only in the sense that Moriarty may not be as powerful as he has led Dr. Barnabus and others to believe. Many people, as we know, overestimate themselves and their influence upon the world. There is a definite possibility, I should think, that this Moriarty has sought you out to taunt you because he wishes to feel important. You are a well-respected man, Mr. Holmes. Could it be that Moriarty simply wishes for you to think that you have found this great mastermind?

"I hope that I do not offend you when I speak in such a manner. You know that you are my friend and my loyalty to you is absolute, but it is that loyalty that compels me to speak. I know that not all of our cases challenge you. Miss Georgiana Darcy was such a one. I took on the case because you did not find it challenging enough for your mind. I can understand that. But could it be that, in your desperation to find a case that is a worthy puzzle for you to solve, you are making this man as greater than he is so that you might create for yourself the challenge that you have always craved, your great hidden adversary?"

Mr. Holmes was silent for a moment. I was grateful once again for our close friendship and for the regard in which Mr. Holmes held me. I knew that what I was saying was not something that he would tolerate hearing from anyone else. Mr. Holmes liked to think himself, despite occasional evidence, as in control of his obsession with intellectual exercises and puzzles. I knew that this was not always the case. He grew inordinately bored and frustrated when there were not cases to solve. His intake of smoking went up, and he grew restless and irritable, pacing back and forth and scaring Mrs. Hudson and generally making a nuisance of himself. I did not think it far off that someone could easily dupe him into thinking there was a criminal mastermind playing puppets with the powers of Europe when there was no such person.

"You raise a good point, Miss Bennet. It is true, there is a possibility that this is all smoke and mirrors. The man who calls himself Moriarty may be nothing more than a lower-rate criminal who wishes to think himself as important and influential. It could be that the persona of Moriarty was created in order to distract from a real crime and to keep me occupied in a fruitless chase. Or Dr. Barnabus could be completely right and there is a very intelligent, very dangerous man who is trying to cause chaos in our land for some unknown reason.

"However, we will not know until we try to seek him out. The answer, whatever it may be, is not worth so much to me as the hunt. I am the dog that does not eat its meat once it catches it. It is the chase of it, picking up its scent and tracking it through the dark woods, that compels me and draws me in.

"With that in mind, my next step is to pluck the strings of this spider's web, so to speak. The spider, as you may well know, will not move from its hiding spot until it senses the movement of a fly upon its web. Then it will scuttle out and strike."

I was, in fact, aware of this bit of information. It was a great pastime among many people in my social class to spend time in the great outdoors and making sketches of all that they saw. In going on walks and rides and sketching, many people I knew had observed and told me about this phenomenon. I found it brutal, but also fascinating.

Mr. Holmes continued. "But did you know that there are certain spiders that hunt other spiders? These spiders seek out a spider web, and when they do, they have a cunning way of plucking the strings so that it imitates the struggles of a trapped fly. The unwary spider, thinking it has dinner, crawls out and the predatory spider pounces and eats it.

"It is our job, then, to pluck the strings. We must lure the spider out of his lair to find out what kind of creature he is. Is he a mirage? A mastermind? A phony? The only way to find out is to draw him out."

"You must realize, Mr. Holmes, the sort of danger this may put you in," I reminded him. "This might provoke actions like those Moriarty has already set against you, such as Dr. Barnabus and his circus."

"I am willing to take such risks," Mr. Holmes pronounced. "If the man is truly a criminal – and there is something suspect going on, Miss Bennet, you cannot deny that – then I will do whatever it takes to bring him to justice. There are many kinds of criminals that should not be allowed to go free, Miss Bennet. There are some with whom I fear the men of Scotland Yard deal too roughly. But most of them have earned their punishment. A man such as this? The kind of man that Moriarty seems to be shaping up to be? I cannot rest until such a man is behind bars where he belongs. If that means that I put myself at risk, then it only means that life is going to get a little more exciting."

I could only laugh to myself at that, although not out loud. Only Mr. Holmes would take the possibility of danger and see it as something exciting to spice up the humdrum of his daily life.

"Of course, this might put you in danger," Mr. Holmes noted.

"Mr. Holmes," I stated. "I am not going to enter into this argument again with you. I understand and I appreciate that you wish for me to be safe. But just as you recently affirmed that you are my friend, so I am yours. I value you and your teachings, but not simply because I am curious or because you are a good detective. Despite your flaws – and you do have them, Mr. Holmes, as do I – I know that you are a good person. You're even an enjoyable person to be around."

Mr. Holmes snorted.

"At times," I amended. "But still. I will not abandon you, just as you have promised not to abandon me. I cannot demand reassurances from you of friendship and then turn my back on you when you might need it."

I paused, worrying that I had become rather too worked up. It had been an emotional few days, what with discovering my own prejudice against Mr. Darcy, handling my mother, and now worrying about my own friendship with Mr. Holmes. I did not want to become emotional in front of Mr. Holmes. I knew how he grew irritated at the extreme emotions of others, and I wanted to be seen as a rational creature. Besides, I suspected that rationality was what would be needed if we were to venture forth into this scheme to draw our possible enemy out of hiding.

Mr. Holmes thought for a moment, his brows drawing together. "Very well," he pronounced. "You seem determined, Miss Bennet, and I know that you are not one to let a little thing such as the opinion of a man stand in your way." He smiled at me at that. "If you are set on your course, then I shall appreciate your assistance. Your insights into human nature are always helpful, and with two hands and two sets of eyes we can accomplish more than I could on my own."

I smiled back at him and nodded. "I presume the first course of action would be to sort through all of these papers?" I asked, gesturing at the stacks.

"Yes. We must get them on the wall and sort out a timeline and locations and connections between them all. Then we can begin to eliminate such things which are superfluous or not actually a part of the man's scheme."

It looked like it would be daunting work, but I was eager to begin. Like Mr. Holmes, I enjoyed the chase. I liked the idea of taking the puzzle pieces and putting them together until they fit and created a complete picture.

Perhaps it was silly of me, but I had also found some new confidence in myself. Mr. Holmes had reaffirmed his sincerity in our friendship and his dependence upon my assistance. Mr. Darcy had apologized and admitted that he thought I could run a detective service on my own without anyone's help. And my mother and I had come to an understanding.

I was excited to move forward on this. I had confidence in my ability to weather the future in whatever form it took. Whatever this Moriarty turned out to be, or rather whomever, I knew that Mr. Holmes and I could tackle him together.

THE END

About the Author

Amelia works as a librarian and lives in an idyllic Cotswold village in England with Darcy, her Persian cat. She has been a Jane Austen fan since childhood but only in later life did she discover the glory and gory of a cozy mystery book. She has drafted many different cases for Holmes and Bennet to solve together.

Visit www.amelialittlewood.com for more details.

KEEP READING...

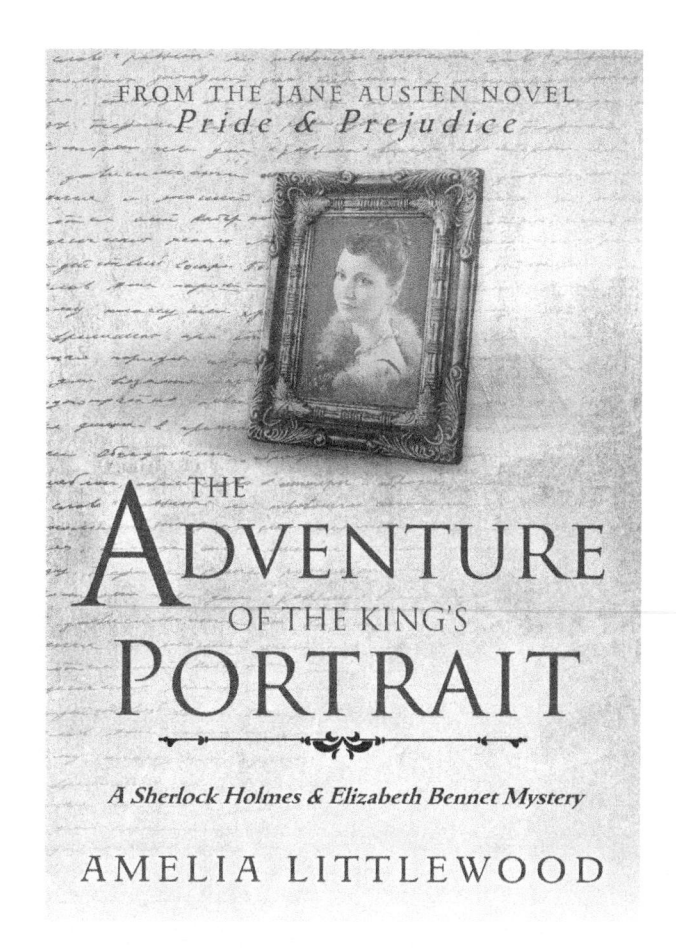

FROM THE JANE AUSTEN NOVEL
Pride & Prejudice

THE ADVENTURE OF THE KING'S PORTRAIT

A Sherlock Holmes & Elizabeth Bennet Mystery

AMELIA LITTLEWOOD

Has Sherlock holmes met his intellectual match in the form of Irene Adler?

CYANIDE PUBLISHING

Made in United States
Orlando, FL
13 February 2025